AURA, AURA

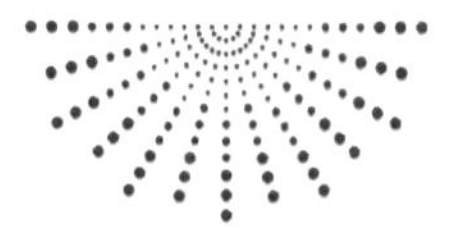

ALICIA RADES

Produced in the United States of America.
Published by Crystallite Publishing LLC.
Edited by Emerald Barnes.
Cover Design by Christian Bentulan.

CHAPTER ONE

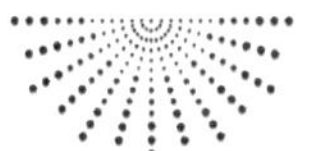

I'd forgotten how dark Aurora High could be, and I wasn't just talking about the vomit-colored tile and bad lighting. When I walked through the doors the first morning of my senior year, dull auras overwhelmed my senses. It was in stark contrast to the bright, vibrant colors I'd become used to over the summer while hanging out at the lake. There, people's auras glowed blue and green, colors of serenity and balance. Here, shades of brown emanated lack of confidence, confusion, and discouragement. I noticed several students surrounded in a dark shade of green, indicating jealousy and low self-esteem. High school was a bitch, and we all knew it.

I took a deep breath and headed toward the table my friends sat at, the same one we'd called home since freshman year. I held my head high. I wasn't going to let everyone else's mood bring me down.

"Katie, over here!" Briana called, standing on her toes and waving me over to our table. Her aura glowed her usual red, communicating her energy and adventure—and her temperament.

Beside her, Lisa smiled at me as I sat. Her blue aura hadn't changed a bit since I last saw her. The calming color suited her well as it showed her charismatic and intelligent side.

As I analyzed my friends' auras, curiosity got the better of me. I glanced down at my hand. The same purple I'd become so accustomed to appeared as a haze surrounding my flesh. It represented an intuitive, loyal personality. It also meant I was unlucky in love. Yay me.

"Hey, girls," I greeted, setting my purse on the floor beside me. "How was your summer?"

Lisa opened her mouth to answer, but Briana cut in before she could. "First things first. Have you seen the new guy?" Her eyes darted between mine and Lisa's. Disbelief fell over her face when she realized we had no idea who she was talking about. "Seriously? Camden Cooper. I told you about him last week."

"Well, you never shut up, so sometimes it's hard to keep up," Lisa teased as she peeled open a granola bar and bit into it.

"Oh, stop." Briana swatted at her. "You remember, don't you, Katie?" She turned to me.

"What, me?" I exchanged a glance with Lisa. "No, seriously. I must have blocked that out. Why should we care?"

Briana rolled her eyes and shifted in her seat. "Um, because he's *hot*. And we haven't had a new kid in our class for, like, two years."

"And?" I dragged out the word.

"And I call *dibs*."

"You can't just call dibs," Lisa told her. 'He's a person, not a piece of cake."

"Trust me," Briana insisted. "He's better than cake, and he's probably not even human. He's like a god or something."

Lisa and I rolled our eyes in sync.

"He can't be that good," I told her as I reached across the table to sweep up Lisa's granola crumbs. My friends had learned by now that I couldn't stand crumbs. They no longer questioned my obsessive need to keep them out of sight.

"What part of 'trust me' don't you understand?" Briana gritted her teeth.

Lisa didn't give me a chance to answer. "How do you know how hot he is?"

"Um…the Internet," Briana said like it was obvious.

"He moved in next door to Austin, who told me about him. Believe me, you'll know him when you see him."

"Well, geez," Lisa teased. "It sounds like you two are practically soul mates."

I laughed, but Briana didn't seem to notice.

"We could be. Austin and him are already friends, so I have an in since I'm a family member and all."

"You're cousins," Lisa pointed out. "It's not like Austin's your brother and the new guy will be over at your house all the time or something."

While Lisa talked, my heart sank. So the new guy didn't even have to *try* to fit in. He just walked in here his senior year with everything figured out while I had to go through two months of freshman hell before finding Lisa and Briana when I was new here. I already hated the guy.

The bell rang, shutting Briana up for the first time that morning. I rose from my seat and slung my purse—that doubled as my book bag—over my shoulder. I walked by the trash on my way to my locker to toss away the crumbs in my hand.

As students filtered down the halls, my attention turned back to the auras I'd been studying earlier. Pops of color showed up here and there, but in general, seeing the student population as a whole was depressing.

Coming from a line of aura readers didn't make high school any easier.

I couldn't help but mutter under my breath. "Welcome to Aurora High, one stop from Hell."

By the end of first period, I decided this year wasn't going to be *that* bad. I mean, it could only be as bad as I made it, and it was actually exciting to see people again. Plus, our semester English project sounded like it was going to be a lot of fun.

"Miss Miller."

I stilled at the sound of my name. The rest of my classmates shuffled out the door while I turned to Mr. Morgan.

"You didn't sign the attendance sheet." The corners of his lips turned down. Despite this, his aura remained a vibrant orange, showing his honest and kind heart.

"Oh, sorry! It must have missed me." I quickly pulled the pencil out from the spiral in my notebook and clicked on the end of it.

Mr. Morgan handed me the clipboard, turning his frown into an encouraging smile. It took a few moments to find my name, but once I did, I quickly checked it off.

"You have a good school year, Miss Miller," Mr. Morgan called as I hurried toward the door.

"You, too." I glanced back at him in a friendly gesture, but I worried I wouldn't have enough time to make it to my locker and then to my next class before the bell rang.

I spun around just in time to slam into something hard, and my books flew from my hands. It took one glance at the open textbook with its pages planted into the floor for me to instantly fall to my knees and snatch it up. I smoothed down the pages. Crap. If I ruined this textbook, I'd owe the school a ton of money I didn't have. I inspected the corners of the book, but it didn't seem too damaged.

"Here," a deep voice said. Someone shoved my purple notebook in my face.

I took it, briefly wondering where my pencil had gone. I glanced around the hall and noticed it about four feet in front of me. Before I could rise from my knees to claim it, a pair of white sneakers came down to crush it. Students hurried so fast to second period that no one seemed to notice. And that was my best pencil. Lovely.

A wave of frustration fell over me. Not only was my favorite pencil now ruined, but there was no way I was making it to second period on time. Just what I needed, a tardy on the first day of school.

"You okay?" the same voice asked.

I sighed. "I'm fine." I stretched forward to grab my pencil. The poor thing didn't stand a chance. I'd have to go back to those cheap yellow pencils I had stashed in my locker.

"You sure?"

"Yes. There's just no point in rushing now that I'm going to be late for class anyway."

"In that case, you might as well ditch."

I gave a light laugh. "I'd ditch my whole senior year if I could get away with it."

As I readjusted my belongings in the crook of my elbow, I finally turned to look at the guy I'd bumped into. My heart nearly stopped, and not because he was drop-dead gorgeous. He may have looked like a god as Briana had said—with bright blue eyes and perfectly symmetrical features—but there was definitely something wrong with this Camden guy.

"I could walk you to class and let your teacher know it was my fault," he offered.

"No, that's okay." I ducked my head and started toward my locker two halls away.

Camden's footsteps followed behind mine. I increased my pace. Only a few students remained in the hall, so I had no one to slow me down.

"Well, would you let me make it up to you somehow?

I was the one who bumped into you." He fell into step beside me. With his long legs, he probably didn't even realize I was practically racing now.

"No, really," I insisted, keeping my gaze down. "It's okay."

As we neared the next hall, I made the snap decision to head to my right toward my science class instead of to my locker to grab a new notebook. I figured we wouldn't be taking any notes today anyway, and I needed a quick escape. To my surprise, Camden followed down the hall with me. My frustration quickly turned to panic. All the other students had already filtered into their classrooms.

"Why are you following me?" I snapped before I could stop myself. My gaze fixed on the open doorway to room 113, my second period class.

"I'm not following you," he defended. "I'm going to class."

I stopped just outside the door. "Well, this is my class, so I guess I'll see you around." I finally glanced up at him again, praying I would *not* be seeing him around any time soon.

A smile stretched across his face. "Mine, too. Looks like we share second period." He pushed past me and into the science lab just as the bell rang.

I let out a groan and slipped in behind him. Briana waved to me from the back.

"Were you just talking to Camden?" she asked under her breath as I took the seat beside her. The chatter around the room nearly drowned out her words.

"Not really?" I said it like it was a question.

"Isn't he hot?" She tossed her curls over her shoulder and stared across the room at Camden, who'd taken a front row seat next to Austin.

"I guess so…"

She managed to peel her eyes off the back of Camden's head. "But…?" she prodded.

I spoke slowly as I tried to come up with a response. "But…you called dibs, so I'm not allowed to look at him like that."

Briana patted my back in show. "You're a good friend."

Mr. Abbott rose from his desk and stood at the front of the room. Everyone went silent, and I was thankful for this. What else would I have said to Briana? I certainly couldn't have told her the truth. I didn't even want to consider it myself. It made no sense. Yet as I stole another glance Camden's way, there was no denying it.

Camden Cooper didn't have an aura.

CHAPTER TWO

I spent the next two periods contemplating what was up with Camden and his aura. The only thing I could think of was that he didn't have a soul. And, okay, I didn't know *everything* there was to know about souls and stuff, but that had to be bad news, right?

Worry continued to taunt me as I entered the cafeteria for lunch. I tried to put Camden out of my mind, but the whole having-no-aura thing really bothered me.

"Ugh," Lisa complained when I met her in the lunch line. "I already have homework for history. What about you?"

I looked up from the nail I was picking at. "No, no homework yet. The morning was pretty boring so far."

Except for Camden, I thought to myself. I couldn't

help but scan the lunch line for him. Maybe I'd made a mistake. Maybe he did have an aura and it just blended into the blue lockers behind him. I tried to remember if there'd been blue behind him in the science lab, but I didn't think so. I needed to catch another glimpse of him to make sure, but I didn't spot him in the lunchroom.

"Are you looking for Briana?" Lisa asked. "Did you see where her locker is this year? It's right next to the lunchroom, so she was one of the first in line."

I followed Lisa's gaze to our table, and my gut twisted. Camden sat between Briana and Austin. The corners of his eyes crinkled as he laughed at something Briana had said. Why did *my* friends have to be the ones to befriend the soulless guy?

I stared at Camden, searching for a trace of his aura. When I couldn't find it, I studied the backdrop behind him, wondering if maybe it was blending in, but I knew that wasn't the case. I could see everyone else's aura at our table except his. Camden's eyes locked on mine, and I quickly averted my gaze.

"Maybe we should go off campus for lunch," I suggested to Lisa.

"What?" she squeaked. "No way. The school's serving pizza. It's the best."

I couldn't argue with that. While the school didn't

have the best reputation when it came to food, they did serve pretty great pizza.

But that didn't mean I wanted to eat it next to Camden. The guy freaked me out.

I couldn't meet his eyes as I approached our table with my tray in hand. Instead of sitting in my usual seat in the middle, I took the spot on the end. Lisa glanced at me in question but sat on my right side without a word.

"So, Camden's going to be on the basketball team this year," Briana announced, leaning into him slightly.

The girl tried too hard.

I kept my gaze on my pizza and cut it into small squares with my fork, but I caught Camden throw Briana a nervous glance.

"I said I'd try out," he clarified. "I wasn't on my old school's team last year, so I may not make the team this year."

"Oh, don't worry. Our school is so small everyone gets on the team," Briana told him. "Besides, you're really tall, so you must be good."

"That doesn't mean anything," I heard myself say.

Wow. Where did that come from? Did I really doubt this guy's athletic ability? Though, maybe he'd traded his soul for his supposed basketball talent and good looks. As far as I knew, demons couldn't actually make deals like that, but a shiver ran down my spine when I considered it as a very real possibility.

"She's right. Height has nothing to do with it."

I was so surprised to hear Camden agree with me that I looked up for the first time.

He stared at me with a smirk on his face. Briana's jaw dropped in shock like she couldn't believe this conversation was taking place.

"Talent comes with hard work and dedication," Camden said. He shot a sideways glance at Briana, but that smirk on his face remained. It was like he was inviting me to take a stab at her.

I couldn't resist. "Yeah, Briana. I'm sure you weren't born with a natural talent for flirting, yet here you are."

Her jaw dropped even further. "I am *not* a flirt."

"Keep telling yourself that," Austin joked from next to Camden.

Briana rolled her eyes, and Lisa laughed from beside me.

I caught one more glance at Camden. He ignored his uneaten food and didn't even pretend he wasn't looking at me.

Briana must have noticed, too. "She's weird with food," she explained, glancing at the fork in my hand.

Except I didn't think Camden was looking at me because I ate pizza with a fork. I wasn't sure what it meant, but the weight of his stare sent an odd sensation to settle in my gut.

Briana approached me at my locker after lunch. "Why were you so rude at lunch today?"

I clicked my locker shut and fell into step beside her. "I didn't mean it. You know I was only poking fun of you."

"I didn't mean about me. Everyone knows I'm a flirt. But why were you so rude to Camden?"

"I—" I paused. I didn't think I'd been *that* rude. He, at least, didn't seem to mind.

"It's not just what you said," Briana complained. "It's what you didn't say."

"What do you mean?"

Briana dodged around a couple that had stopped in the middle of the hall. "Well, you didn't even welcome him to the school or anything, and you hardly talked all lunch. It's like you were avoiding him or something."

I couldn't exactly avoid him when we sat at the same table, I thought, but I didn't tell her this.

"I didn't know I was obligated to do any of that," I said instead.

"I wouldn't say *obligated*, but do you, like, not like

him or something?" She slowed her pace outside our fifth period classroom and turned to stare at me.

Why does she even care? I wondered. *Probably because she thinks she's going to date him,* another voice answered.

"He's fine," I lied. "It's just—"

What was I supposed to say? It's not like Briana knew I could see auras or would believe me if I told her Camden didn't have one.

"Just what?" she asked.

I settled on the easiest explanation. "I just…don't know him yet. You know I'm not good with strangers."

She nodded slowly like she didn't buy it. "Just try to get along, okay?"

"Yeah, sure," I agreed before following her into the math room.

I groaned internally when I spotted Camden in the front row. Briana slid into a seat beside him, and I knew I had no choice but to join her. I took the chair behind her, all the while dreading the sickening feeling in my stomach that told me I was going to have to get along with Camden whether I liked it or not.

I was relieved to find I didn't have any more classes with Camden the rest of the day. As much as I wanted to forget about the guy and put him out of my mind, I couldn't. He was so strange, almost in an intriguing way that made me want to investigate.

He's probably dangerous, I told myself. And that was exactly why I shouldn't investigate. Just because I could see auras didn't mean I had a responsibility to somehow fix them. I slammed my locker at the end of the day, set on this decision, but when I turned around, I found myself face-to-face with icy blue eyes.

"Holy hell!" I took a step back to keep from ramming into him for a second time.

Camden smiled down at me. "Hi, Katie."

"Um, hi." I dropped my head and stepped around him, following the flow of traffic to the front doors of the school. How did he know my name? Had I mentioned it earlier? I couldn't remember.

"What are you up to after school?" Camden paced beside me.

"I'm, uh, going home," I told him shyly.

"Oh? So you're not busy?"

"Actually, I planned to work on some homework," I lied.

"Homework on the first day of school?"

"Yeah. In history."

We stepped out into the bright sun. A warm breeze touched my skin. The auras I spotted from students around me seemed to glow brighter in the pleasant weather.

"Well, that can't take you all night. Do you want to hang out?"

I whirled around so fast that Camden nearly ran into me. "What?" I bit the word sharper than I intended.

"I asked if you wanted to hang out."

"Wh—but—" I stammered, taking a step back to distance myself from him. His lack of aura freaked me out enough as it was. The invitation to hang out only made him seem creepier than I initially thought. "Why?"

Camden shrugged. "You seem cool."

I blinked rapidly in surprise. "I'm not."

Camden laughed like he thought I was kidding. I wasn't.

"Really," I stated confidently, "I'm busy tonight. Maybe some other time."

He nodded slowly. "Okay."

"Yeah…um…I'll see you." I quickly rushed off toward my car and locked myself inside before I ever heard a response. I sat in the junker for a good five minutes. By the time I caught my breath and raised my head, nearly the whole parking lot was clear. I took a deep breath and shifted into drive, trying to shake off the strange encounter the whole ride home.

$\mathcal{I}$ hadn't lied about having history homework, but it wasn't due until the end of the week, and I really didn't feel like working on it now. Instead, I spread out a blanket in the back yard and read a book. I couldn't get past the part where the vampire asked the new girl at school out. It felt too much like what had happened earlier with Camden. Sure, he was the one who was new at school, and I was pretty sure he wasn't a vampire, but it had me second guessing the whole thing.

I closed my eyes and rolled onto my back. The sun glowed brightly above me, warming my exposed skin. *Maybe Camden is a vampire,* I thought. It wasn't like I believed in vampires, but it could explain why he didn't have an aura with the whole soulless and undead thing. And it made more plausible sense that he wanted to hang out so he could murder me for my blood rather than actually being interested in my company.

If not a vampire, then what?

Almost instantly, another thought entered my mind, but I quickly pushed it away. I thought I was past the days of thinking I saw demons wherever I went.

Don't be stupid, Katie, I told myself.

The hum of my father's engine pulling into the driveway brought me back to the present. I sighed and stood, gathering my book and blanket from the grass.

"How was your first day of school?" he asked when I entered the kitchen from the back door. The fridge buzzed when he opened it to deposit the gallon of milk he'd picked up on his way home. I smiled at the sight of his yellow aura.

I shrugged. "Same old, same old. How was work?"

He shrugged. "Same old, same old. Did you make dinner yet?"

I shook my head and placed my book on the table. I tossed my blanket by the back door since I figured I'd probably use it again tomorrow. I wanted to enjoy as much of the warm weather as I could before autumn hit.

"I can start on it, though," I offered.

"Do you want any help?" he asked.

I laughed. "No, it's fine. I know cooking isn't your thing."

His face fell. "I know. I just thought—"

"You can sit at the table and keep me entertained." I smiled. "Or set the table."

He nodded and reached into the cupboard for three plates. He still always set out a place for Mom like he thought she might walk through the door and join us for dinner. I didn't pretend to understand it.

I scoured the cupboards for lasagna ingredients, feeling slightly bad about denying his help again. When Mom died, I quickly learned that Dad was a terrible cook, so I'd taken over a few years back. He seemed more than happy about it, and I rather enjoyed cooking.

"So, tell me more about your first day at school," Dad said, taking a seat at the table.

"There's not much to say." I stretched up to retrieve the lasagna pan from one of the cabinets. "We just went over the syllabus and stuff in every class. We get to choose our lab partners in science, so Briana and I are going to be together. There's a new guy, Camden, but he's kind of weird."

"Oh?" Dad raised his eyebrows. "Weird how?"

I continued my way around the kitchen with my back to him. What could I say to that? I didn't talk to my dad about auras, not anymore. Mom had been the one to teach me how to read them. Dad didn't really care at the time, but after what happened to Mom, he was scared I'd get myself into trouble. It didn't matter how many times I reminded him that what happened to her could happen to anyone, aura reader or not. He still didn't like the thought of me following in Mom's footsteps, so I practiced my gift in secret.

I blinked away the tears that formed when my mom crossed my mind. In the reflection of the stove, I noticed my dad leaning forward, still waiting for an answer about Camden.

I shrugged. "I don't know. He's just weird. He asked me out earlier."

"Hold up," Dad laughed. "So the new guy asked you out, and your reaction is that it's *weird*? Isn't that a good thing?"

I turned to him, a smirk on my face. "Do you want me to date?"

"God, no. You're not dating until you're thirty."

I laughed and turned back to the lasagna noodles. "I don't know. Just forget I said anything."

"Katie." Dad's voice was firm, getting me to look back at him. "This guy isn't giving you trouble, is he?"

"No, Dad. You know I'm just weird around strangers."

He nodded like it all made sense.

After today, I wasn't sure what made sense anymore.

After dinner, I made my way upstairs to my bathroom and climbed into the tub. The hot water and lavender scent from my bubble bath helped soothe me. For the first time all day, I was able to put Camden from my mind.

Unfortunately, he returned to my thoughts when I made it back to my bedroom. I sighed and tossed my wet towel on the bed. After slipping on my pajamas, I pulled open the top drawer of my dresser and dug out the candle and matches I kept there. Turning to the window, I opened it a crack so Dad wouldn't smell the candle. I dropped to the floor cross-legged and lit the wick. Sucking in a deep breath, I channeled my energy into my chest and let it all out through the exhale. The tension in my shoulders eased with every breath.

When I felt relaxed enough, I crawled to the edge of my bed and reached beneath it. My hand fell around a leather object. I pulled the spell book out from under the bed and hugged it to my chest. I hadn't used it much since Mom died, but I still cherished it.

My father's footsteps creaked in the living room,

pulling my attention away from the book. The sound of his bare feet against the hardwood floor faded under me until I heard the thud of his bedroom door shut. Even though I knew he wouldn't bother me, I tiptoed over to my door and locked it. Just to be safe.

Returning to my spot on the floor in front of the candle, I opened the spell book and paged through it. I flipped past at least a dozen spells and incantations Mom never got a chance to teach me—because I wasn't ready, she'd said—before I found the one I was looking for.

The protection spell was simple. All I had to do was write the name of the person I wanted to be protected from on a piece of paper and burn it while I spoke the incantation. My purse sat next to me, so I reached into it and pulled out a pen and a scrap receipt. I tore the receipt in half and then scrawled Camden's name on it.

For a moment, I simply stared down at the writing. I didn't *really* need to do this. It's not like Camden was a danger to me or anything. Yet I still couldn't get past the strange feeling I got when I met him today. A lump formed in my throat when I thought about it.

"Better to be safe than sorry," I told myself in a whisper.

Then I held out the paper to the flame and chanted the incantation under my breath. When the paper reduced to nothing but ash, a sense of confidence overcame me. I blew out the candle and placed my supplies back in their proper spots. I crawled into bed and stared up at the ceiling, feeling slightly guilty about using the spell book on one of my classmates.

CHAPTER FOUR

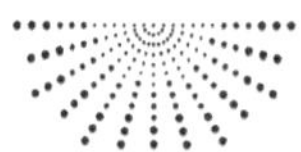

Over the next few days, it became clear to me that the protection spell worked. I kept my distance from Camden, and he didn't try to talk to me either. He even went off campus for lunch with Austin, so I didn't have to sit by him. Briana became frustrated with sitting in the front row for math because Mrs. Taylor always called on her, so we moved to the back while Camden stayed in the front. I counted it a blessing.

All my efforts to avoid him appeared useless on Friday after school. When I shut my locker and turned to head to my car at the end of the day, I found Camden blocking my path. I instantly took a step back.

"You have *got* to stop doing that," I said a bit too harshly.

"I'm sorry," he said with a kind smile. For some reason, it made me want to hurl. I just couldn't read the guy.

I stepped around him, but I couldn't seem to hurry out of the school fast enough. Students fled from the halls so quickly that there was no longer much of a crowd to hide myself in. I could sense the heat of Camden's body next to mine, but his soul energy seemed non-existent.

"I'm sorry," he repeated. "I didn't see Briana or Austin, so I was just wondering if you knew about their plans for tonight."

"Wh—what plans?" I stammered.

Damn my friends. I should have realized they'd invite Camden to our fire tonight. Briana still had her dibs on him, and he and Austin had apparently become good friends. I couldn't exactly skip out since it was our first fire of the school year, and we wouldn't have many left before the weather got too cold. I'd just have to avoid Camden like usual. That couldn't be too hard.

"Austin said you guys have campfires every weekend at the lake?" It was more a question than a statement.

"Yeah, we do," I told him stupidly as we pushed through the doors into the sun.

"I didn't get the address. Do you have it?"

I almost had the urge to tell him to ask someone else.

Clearly, I wasn't interested in being friends, and he could have easily texted Austin or Briana for it. But I didn't want to be rude either.

I squinted up at him, the sun nearly blinding me. "Um, if you just head out on Lake Drive, it's the second house on the right past the bait shop. It's the white one with blue shutters. You can't miss it."

"Okay. Thanks," he said. "I'll see you tonight, then?"

I nodded. "Yeah."

Camden gave a slight wave and then turned to head to the parking lot. I decided to give him a minute so I wouldn't have to walk beside him. As I stared after him, I thought I saw a glimpse of something.

No, I told myself. I squinted harder, but he was too far away now. Yet I *swore* I saw some sort of dark aura around him, only it seemed off center. *It must be my eyes playing tricks on me from the sun,* I figured. But if it *had* been real, having a dark aura was better than having no aura at all, wasn't it? As I headed to my car, I knew I didn't have an answer to that.

"How do I look?" Briana greeted me at the bottom of the stairs when I entered her house. She spun in a circle for show.

"Isn't it a little…short?" I didn't know how else to break it to her.

Briana smoothed down the pink mini dress. "When there are boys involved, nothing's too short." She eyed me up and down, scrutinizing my long jeans and zip-up hoodie.

"You're going to get cold," I pointed out. I really wished she would change. I knew she wore the dress to get Camden's attention, but I worried about her. I could only cast a protection spell for myself, but I still didn't want her getting involved with someone who didn't have a soul.

"Relax," she said. "I have plenty of clothes upstairs I can change into if I get cold."

I opened my mouth to say more, but I quickly snapped it shut. If I tried to say something to her about avoiding Camden, it would only drive her closer to him.

"You okay?" Concern entered Briana's voice.

"What? Yeah. I'm fine. Here." I shoved my container in her direction. "It's all I had at home."

She peeked into the container. "Ooh, rice crispy treats. Thanks for bringing something. My dad already has the grill going. Did you want a brat or a hamburger? Or both?"

I followed Briana to the kitchen. "A brat is fine, thanks."

"Dad! Katie wants a brat," she shouted through the open French doors that led to the back patio.

"Okay," he shouted back.

A light knock came from the front door a moment before it creaked open. "Hello?" Lisa's voice traveled down the hall.

"In here," Briana called back.

My friends and I gathered food and then headed to the patio to join Austin and a few of his friends. I was relieved to find that Camden hadn't made it yet.

Fifteen minutes later, I was laughing so hard at one of Austin's jokes that I nearly choked on my soda. It was at that moment that Camden decided to make an appearance. I coughed a few more times and then went silent.

Austin hopped up from his chair. "Hey, man."

"Hey." Camden came around the side of the house. He spoke quietly like he was tired. "Am I late?"

"Nah, there's plenty of food left," Austin told him.

"Hey, Camden," Briana called, waving him over. "We saved you a seat."

I quickly shoved the rest of my food in my mouth and then stood. "I'm going for seconds," I announced, even though no one seemed to notice. I was actually pretty full, but I didn't want to end up sitting right next to him.

I slipped inside and tossed my paper plate in the garbage. Sighing, I reached for one of the rice crispy bars and pulled it apart before popping a chunk in my mouth.

"Hey," a deep voice came from the doorway.

I whirled around in surprise.

Camden furrowed his brow. "You okay?"

I shoved another piece of rice crispy in my mouth. "Yeah. I'm fine. You?"

"Yeah, just a headache. I get them all the time." He shrugged like it was no big deal.

I leaned against the counter uncomfortably but kept my eyes on the rice crispy bar I was peeling apart. The marshmallow goo left a string between the pieces. I glanced up just in time to catch Camden staring.

"What?" I asked curiously.

He blinked a few times before answering. "Nothing. You just…remind me of someone."

I nodded slowly but took the opportunity in the silence to slip out the door. When I looked back for just a split second, I could have sworn I saw that dark aura around him again. I was already moving so fast that I didn't stop to confirm. Instead, I headed down to the fire pit near the lake shore. The fire wasn't even going yet, and everyone else was still up by the house eating, but I didn't see the harm in escaping.

"Heads up!" someone called from down the beach.

I glanced up just in time to see a volleyball headed straight toward my head. I did the only thing I could do. I smacked it out of the way. The ball soared in a new direction, bouncing off the end of the dock and landing in the water. It slowly floated farther and farther from the dock.

"Really, Katie?" A sophomore named Drake rushed up to me with a disappointed look on his face.

He lived next door to Briana and almost always held some sort of party at his place on the weekends. This weekend, it was beach volleyball. I always figured it was his way of trying to show Briana up. The other sophomores around the net groaned and stared out at the water as the ball distanced itself from shore.

"What are we going to do now?" Drake complained, crossing his short arms.

"You could jump in after it," I suggested with a shrug.

"To hell with that. You go get it. You're the one who hit it in the lake anyway."

I continued on my way to the fire pit and sat. There was usually no reasoning with this kid. "No way. You're the one who hit it at my head."

"It's not like I meant it." Drake stood next to me, but even with me sitting down, he was only a few inches taller.

"I didn't mean it, either," I defended.

He turned to yell at his friends, who hadn't stopped groaning. "Hang on!" His attention focused back on me. "Are you going to go get our ball or not?"

I glanced down at his shorts and bare feet. "I'm not jumping in the lake. I'm fully clothed. You're only wearing shorts, and you can go inside and change if you don't want to be wet."

Drake let out a puff of air like I was being unfair. And, okay, maybe I was, but it didn't matter what I did. Nothing would please him.

"What's going on?" Camden's voice came from behind me.

I twisted to find him followed by Briana and Lisa, who both looked at me with concern. We all knew that if Drake made an appearance, it was bad news.

"Katie threw my ball into the lake and won't go get it," Drake complained like he was tattling to his parents.

"I didn't mean to," I repeated.

Camden glanced between Drake and me like he couldn't believe we were actually fighting about this. "Okay. There's a simple solution."

"And what's that?" Drake challenged.

Camden was already slipping off his shoes and socks. When his shirt came off, Briana drew in an auditory breath. Camden didn't say anything as he hurried to the end of the dock and jumped in the water. I stared wide-eyed after him. A second later, his head poked up over the surface, and he swam to retrieve the ball. Water pooled on the dock when he climbed out of the lake. He shook the water from his hair and tossed the ball in Drake's direction. Drake fumbled and just barely caught it before running back to his friends without so much as a thank you.

"Oh my god." Briana rushed toward Camden. "You must be freezing. Let's get you inside and dry you off."

I remained speechless, still not quite believing that he bailed me out of that one. On his way past me, Camden grabbed his t-shirt and shoes. He caught my eye as he stood, and I couldn't help but mouth a *thank you* to him.

Maybe Camden wasn't quite as bad as I thought he was.

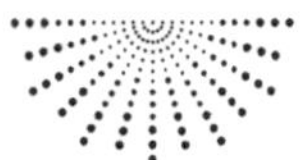

CHAPTER FIVE

That night, I arrived home so late that Dad was already in bed. I considered myself lucky because then I could look through my spell book without worry of being caught. I pulled the ancient thing out from under my bed and clicked on the bedside lamp before crawling under the sheets. I opened the front cover carefully and gently turned the delicate page to the table of contents. Mom had told me the spell book was my grandma's, but I suspected it was much older than that. I didn't think my mom ever knew where Grandma got it, but with how fragile the pages seemed, I could only guess it had more than three owners.

When I couldn't find what I was looking for in the table of contents, I flipped each page one by one, wondering if maybe I'd missed something. I hoped I'd find something that could help me identify evil. That way, I'd know for sure if Camden was dangerous or not. Not having an aura didn't make him evil, did it? I wanted to find out for sure, but there was no such spell in the book.

The following week brought no answers. Briana's obsession with Camden seemed to tone down after he hadn't shown interest in her at our fire on Friday night. Camden and I rarely crossed paths except in the classes we shared and one day at lunch when it was raining and he'd stayed on campus. I hardly thought about him.

I hadn't considered he would notice until he showed up at my locker on Friday after school. My heart nearly jumped out of my chest.

"Is this going to become a regular thing?" I asked, half joking.

Camden ignored the question. "Are you avoiding me?"

I gave a nervous giggle that came out sounding fake. "What? No. Of course not. Why would you think that?" *You don't know anything about me*, I thought to myself. *How would you know what it looks like for me to avoid you?*

"Really? Because even Briana says you act weird around me."

Camden was so close that I felt the urge to take a step back. When I did, the cool of my locker sent a chill down my spine.

"Me? She's the one who gets all weird."

He raised his eyebrows in amusement. "Why would she get weird around me?"

"Um, because she likes you," I said like it was obvious. I mean, the guy had to know.

"Clearly," he said, a bit too confidently if you asked me. He paused for only a beat before asking, "Does that mean you like me, too?"

I ducked my head and hurried down the hall before he could spot the blush rising to my cheeks. "I was *not* implying that."

"Then what is it? Did I do something to offend you?"

I stopped in my tracks, and Camden nearly ran into me. I actually had to put a bit of thought into the question. In truth, he hadn't done *anything*. He was a sweet guy. It was just…

"No, you didn't. I'm just not good with strangers." I hated that that was becoming my go-to excuse. It wasn't even particularly true.

Camden held the door open for me when we reached it. I stepped out of the building into warm air.

"Well, then," he said, "I guess we're just going to have to get to know each other."

I nodded like I agreed, but when I glanced up at him, I noticed he was waiting for more. "What? You mean, like, right now?"

"You're not busy, are you?"

"Well, I—I…" I stammered. I didn't have an excuse.

"Come on." Camden headed toward the parking lot, expecting me to follow. I didn't know what else to do.

"I can't," I told him, hurrying up to reach him. With his long legs, I nearly had to run to catch up. "I, um, have to make dinner for my dad."

"It can wait, can't it?" Camden stopped next to a blue sedan much nicer than my car. "It's okay, Katie."

I glanced between his car and my gray junker in the next row. "What about my car?"

"I can drop you back off here to get it."

I bit my lip nervously.

"Or you can drive it home now and put some dinner in the oven. Then we can hang out for a while. I'll follow you."

I swallowed hard. *Maybe I should get to know him*, I thought. Perhaps it would shed light on the mystery surrounding him.

Camden took my silence as a yes. "Great. I'll see you

in a few." Then he ducked into his vehicle and turned the ignition switch.

I headed over to my car, still wondering what had just happened. Feeling like I had no other choice, I started the engine and led him to my house anyway.

CHAPTER SIX

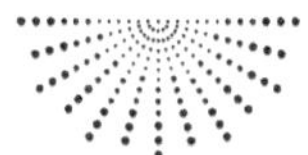

"I should be home by five," I told Camden as I climbed into his passenger seat. "You know, to check on the food." I'd left a roast in the crock pot for my dad. It wouldn't be done for hours, but Camden didn't need to know that.

He nodded and pulled out of the driveway. "That doesn't give us much time to get to know each other, does it?"

I shifted nervously in my seat and stared out the window. "Why do you want to get to know me anyway?" I wanted to shove the words back in my mouth as soon as I spoke. At least I didn't let my other thoughts slip about why my protection spell was no longer working on him. Had it worn off?

Camden shrugged. "You're an interesting person."

How would you know? You don't even know me, I thought. "What gave you that idea?"

He sighed and shifted his hands on the steering wheel. "I can't figure you out."

My brows shot up. *He* couldn't figure *me* out? Had I stepped into some strange alternate reality?

"There's not much to me," I admitted.

He glanced my way for a second before fixing his eyes back on the road. "You're different from other girls."

"You mean I'm not like Briana?" I asked before I could stop myself.

He paused for a moment. "Yeah, I guess."

Silence hung in the air, and I took the moment to consider what he meant. Was he saying he wanted to get to know me because he couldn't figure out why I didn't have a crush on him like all the other girls in school did? If only they knew what I knew about him…

"Once when I was in third grade, I fell off the monkey bars and broke my wrist," Camden announced.

I kept my gaze on the road and spoke slowly. "Okay."

He nudged me with his elbow. "It's part of us trying to get to know each other. Now you tell me something."

"Oh, um, like what?" This time, I looked at him, but as soon as his eyes met mine, I averted my gaze.

"Anything."

"Okay," I started reluctantly, "but only if I get to ask you a question. And you have to answer honestly."

I caught him nod out of the corner of my eye.

"Okay. I'm allergic to bees," I told him. In the brief silence that followed, I contemplated what I might ask him. I couldn't exactly come out and ask why he didn't have an aura. Instead, another question escaped my lips. "What brought you to Aurora High?"

He sucked in a long breath through his teeth like it was a difficult question to answer. "We're here," he said instead, pulling into a gravel parking lot.

"We're going hiking?" I asked stupidly.

"Is there anything else to do in this town?" The question was rhetorical.

"You didn't answer my question," I accused, stepping out of the vehicle.

Camden started toward the trailhead but remained quiet. For a moment, I thought he wasn't going to answer. Finally, he spoke. "It's a long story. The short version? There was a death in my family. It was…a lot to handle. So I moved in with my grandparents as a way to sort of start over."

I nearly tripped over a root in the path as I stared up at Camden's sad eyes. I didn't know what it was about his story, but the way he told it made him seem more—

for lack of a better word—human. Honestly, I'd thought there wasn't much to the guy, but here I found out we had something in common.

"What about you?" he asked, pulling my attention back to the trail. "Briana said you didn't grow up around here."

I pushed my hair out of my face and carefully watched my step. "No, I was new here freshman year." Even though he'd just opened up to me, I couldn't bring myself to tell him about my mom's death. I couldn't tell him about how Dad lost his job from missing too much work afterward and how we couldn't afford our house anymore. I settled with, "My dad got a job at the paper mill."

Camden and I continued down the path, but I couldn't get his confession out of my head. *There was a death in my family.* All I wanted to say was *mine too*, but I choked on the words.

Still, I felt like I had to say *something* to fill the silence. I spit out the first thing I could think of. "So, how do you like living with your grandparents?"

He shrugged and gazed down at the path. "I like living with them, but sometimes I wonder if maybe they'd be better off without me around."

Tension immediately entered the air. Camden wouldn't look at me, as if he realized he'd said too much.

My heart sank as I thought about how those words sounded so much like my mother's.

Stop it, Katie, I told myself. *Not everyone you meet is like your mom. Camden just cares about his grandparents' feelings.*

His tone shifted. "So, tell me. What's your favorite color?"

"Purple," I answered automatically. "Why?"

"I told you. It's all part of us getting to know each other."

"What's yours then?"

The answer couldn't come soon enough. I'd found that most people were drawn to the color of their auras. Sure, their auras changed with their mood, but most people's auras balanced to a specific color for their personality. Since Camden didn't have an aura, I couldn't guess what his favorite color might be.

He shrugged. "I'm not sure. Blue, maybe?"

"You're not sure?" I asked with raised eyebrows.

"There are too many choices."

"Fair point."

The more I talked to Camden, the more I relaxed. Despite his lack of aura, he didn't seem that bad. He even seemed nice. And then, for just a brief moment, the reality of how we were alone in the woods struck me. Could he be playing me and trying to get me alone for some reason? *To kill me for my blood because he's a vampire.* Honestly, I didn't get that feeling from him. Besides, if something bad *did* happen, I had a few incantations up my sleeve that would allow me to defend myself. Mom had made sure those were some of the first ones I'd learned.

Then again, if he was so nice, why didn't he have an aura? I continued down the path with him, hoping he'd reveal the answer soon.

The more we walked, the higher in elevation we climbed. The terrain around here didn't exactly have much variety, but eventually, the trail led to an open area that overlooked our small town. A small bench offered us a place to sit. I tried my best to keep to the edge of my seat so I wouldn't touch him, but I could still sense the heat of his body next to me.

"What's one thing you don't like that everyone else does?" Camden asked, continuing the series of questions meant to help us get to know each other.

I crinkled my nose. "That's a hard one. I guess...I don't like shoes?"

"Shoes?" Camden draped an elbow over the back of the bench and turned to me with an amused expression.

"Yeah. Like, most girls love shoes, and to me, all I need are my tennies." I lifted my legs and twisted my ankles to show him the shoes. They weren't exactly pretty.

"Okay," he said like he understood.

"And you?" I asked.

"Um…video games."

"What is wrong with you?" I feigned shock.

He shrugged. "There are just better things to do with my time."

In that moment, a high-pitched chirping sound caught my attention. "Do you hear that?" I stood and inched toward the sound near the edge of the manicured grass.

"I do," Camden said slowly, rising to join me.

I pulled long blades of grass apart, following the sound of the chirping. Eventually, I parted a section of grass to find the source of the chirping: a small yellow bird.

"Oh, no. I think he might be hurt." I reached down to fold my hands over the small creature. I could feel Camden looking over my shoulder at him. "What should we do with him?"

"Do you think that's maybe his nest?" Camden pointed to a branch above us.

"Maybe." I peeked into my hands at the bird. "I don't think he can fly yet."

"Maybe we should put him back in his nest," he suggested.

Camden reached out his hands, and I placed the bird in them. He gently cupped the small creature in one hand and used a finger to pet its head. The bird folded into a smaller ball and chirped at him.

"Aw, isn't he cute?" Camden asked, holding up the bird to show me one more time.

I nodded. "Be careful with him, okay?"

"I will." He reached up to the branch above us, but he couldn't quite reach it. "Here." He handed the bird back to me.

I wasn't sure how I was going to help since he was several inches taller than me. I cupped the bird in my hands and whispered to it, letting it know it was going to be all right. Camden paced beneath the branch and gazed up at it. Then, in one swift motion, he jumped and caught it. I drew in a surprised breath. Camden pulled himself up until his legs straddled the branch. He scooted himself closer until he could reach the nest. Then he extended his arm down. I stretched up on my toes and placed the bird in his hand. Camden gave the creature another stroke on the head and gently set him back in his nest. I smiled at the victory.

"Coming down," Camden warned.

I hardly had a second to react before I caught the

motion out of the corner of my eye and heard the thud of his feet as he hit the ground. He stumbled slightly and caught himself on my shoulders. His touch made me jump, but he quickly apologized.

"We should maybe get back to the car," he suggested.

"Yeah," I agreed, but I kept my gaze locked on the nest above me.

If Camden was so gentle with the bird and willing to help out wildlife, he had to have a heart of some sort, right? It was the only explanation for his kindness.

On the way back to the car, Camden suggested we play two truths and a lie.

He went first. "One, pizza is my favorite food. Two, I'm the younger of two brothers. Three, I prefer cats to dogs."

"Mmm…" I let out a sigh. They all seemed plausible. Then I recalled how Camden hardly touched his pizza at lunch on the first day of school. "One is a lie," I stated confidently.

A smile crept across his lips. "Nope. Three is the lie. I like dogs."

I nodded slowly, thinking briefly how that didn't make sense to me, but I didn't push it. Instead, I asked, "Does your brother live with your grandparents, too?" Only a moment later did I realize he said his brother was *older* than him so he was probably off at college or something.

"No," he said, dropping his gaze to the path and pressing his lips into a thin line.

"What is it?" I asked.

Camden eyed me curiously. "It's just that you remind me of him a little."

"I do? In what way?"

He shrugged. "Your humor. The way you eat your pizza with a fork and rip apart your rice crispy bars before eating them. I've just never seen anyone else do that."

I laughed. "Well, it's good to know I'm not the only one who's weird with food. Is it my turn? *My* favorite food is cheesecake, I'm an only child, and I too prefer dogs to cats."

Camden thought about it for a moment before answering. "The third one is the lie."

I sighed in defeat. "Yeah."

We spent most of the walk back playing two truths and a lie, allowing us to dig up even more information about each other. By the time we reached the car, I'd nearly forgotten why I was so wary to get to know him in the first place.

"I hope you had fun," he said as he slid into the driver's seat.

I opened the passenger side door. "I did. It was a really nice day for a walk. And I learned a lot more about you than I ever thought I would."

Camden didn't start the car right way, nor did he meet my gaze. "And what do you think?"

"You mean what do I think about you? I think…" I couldn't find the right words. "I think I may have misjudged you." As soon as I admitted it, I realized I meant it. So I'd misjudged him. What did that mean about his aura?

"Does that mean—" Camden stopped mid-sentence and dropped his hands from the steering wheel. He fidgeted slightly in his seat and turned to me. "Two lies and a truth?"

"You mean two truths and a lie."

"No, two lies and a truth." He leaned closer to me. "One, I don't find you interesting at all."

I rolled my eyes and smiled. "Well, that has to be a lie."

He nodded. "Two, you weren't the first girl to catch my eye at Aurora High."

"Um…truth?"

He shook his head and leaned in even closer until I

could feel his hot breath on my face. "That's another lie. Three, I want to kiss you right now."

My breath caught in my chest. My next word came out as a whisper. "Truth?"

His eyes shifted between mine and my lips. My heart beat wildly against my chest in anticipation.

"Truth," he whispered before closing the gap between us and pressing his lips to mine.

CHAPTER SEVEN

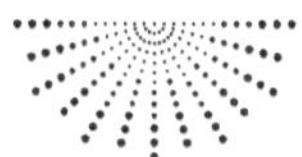

"*I*—I'm sorry," Camden said after a moment, pulling away.

I sucked in a sharp breath, and not just because the kiss left me breathless. When I opened my eyes, I was surprised to find a light red glow just barely illuminating off his skin. For the first time since I'd met him, Camden appeared to have a true colorful aura.

"No," I whispered breathlessly, still mesmerized by the red hue surrounding him that seemed to glow brighter with each passing second. I could only wonder how bright it might grow. "It's okay. You can do that again."

And he did. Camden's lips were soft against mine. He grazed his tongue against my bottom lip, making me want nothing more than to pull him closer to me. I locked my hands around his neck, and his settled on my hips. His warm hands made contact with my bare back, causing me to suck in another breath of surprise. My pulse quickened, and I leaned in even closer to him until he pulled me over the middle console and onto his lap.

I only had a brief moment to wonder what I was doing. I didn't even know the guy. But something that felt this good couldn't be bad, right?

Eventually, Camden pulled away. "You had to be home by five, right?"

I hesitated before answering. "Right." Before I could stop myself, the next words tumbled out of my mouth. "But you could stay for dinner if you want." I situated myself back in my seat and readjusted the hem of my shirt.

"Sounds like fun." Camden put the car into gear and pulled out of the parking lot.

This time on the car ride, I kept my eyes on him as he talked. The red hue I'd seen earlier remained, though it was dimmer than the other auras I was used to. It stayed close to his body, just barely an outline. Could it be that this aura was there all along and I'd just missed it? Or did the kiss change something? The whole ride home, I wondered if it had changed something inside of him or inside of me.

"Thank you," I told Camden as soon as we arrived at my house.

"For what?" He shut off the engine and turned to me.

For helping me see how wrong I was about you. "For taking me on the trails."

"No problem."

"Camden." I stopped him before he could exit the vehicle. I froze, realizing I didn't know what I was going to say. I went the easy route. Instead of saying *anything*, I reached out for him and pulled his lips to mine once again.

He drew away with a smile on his face. That red, passionate aura of his seemed to grow brighter. It was still nothing like I was used to, but at least now I could see it. Why, then, was I still having trouble feeling his soul's energy? Something about him felt cold and empty, despite him seeming so full of life.

"What is it?" Camden asked, reaching up a hand to tuck my hair behind my ear.

I hadn't realized my face had fallen. I glanced away toward the back seat. "I just..."

A shadow caught my eye. I blinked several times, praying I was just imagining things, but the dark haze remained. My entire body tensed. Anger flared inside my veins, anger at *myself* for writing it off, for not seeing it sooner.

"Get inside. Now." The immediate concern was evident in my tone.

"What? Why?" Camden glanced to the back seat, but I knew he wouldn't see it.

"Just do it." I rushed to open my door, and he followed quickly behind.

"What's going on?" His breathing sounded labored, worried, as he pushed through the front door of the house.

I wanted to answer, to give him some sort of explanation, but the words caught in my throat. All I could manage to choke out was a command to stay in the living room. Camden took a seat on the couch, a confused expression fixed on his face, while I turned to head up the stairs two at a time. Curse words escaped from under my breath. I snatched up the spell book from under my bed and gathered my candle and matches from my dresser. I nearly tripped over the area rug in the living room when I returned. Dropping to the floor with purpose, I spread my supplies across the coffee table in front of Camden. I frantically flipped the pages in search of the spell I needed.

"Katie," Camden said firmly. When I didn't answer, he reached out to grab my wrists.

His touch immediately stopped me. I froze, moving

ever so slightly to gaze up at him. Hot tears burned my eyes.

"Katie, what's going on?" He released me.

I blinked several times, and the tears receded. Clearing my throat, I returned my attention to the spell book and flipped the next page carefully. It all made sense now, why he didn't seem to have an aura. I knew now why my protection spell hadn't kept him away. I never needed protection from him in the first place.

My tone wavered. "How long ago did the depression start?"

"What are you talking about?" His voice remained calm, but a hint of confusion was present in it.

"The depression," I stated flatly. "The suicidal thoughts. How long has it been?" I glanced up from the book to assess his reaction once again.

Shock settled over his face. "How do you know about that?"

My pulse quickened, and I swallowed hard. I had no other choice but to be blunt with him. "Because, Camden, you have a demon attached to you. I know because the same thing happened to my mom. Before she killed herself."

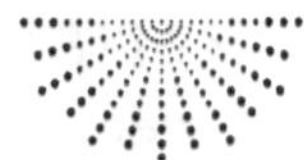

$\mathcal{I}$ couldn't believe I hadn't seen it sooner. But that was the thing about depression. The signs were there, but no one ever took the time to notice them.

Even with my mom, I hadn't noticed her purple aura growing dimmer day by day. The soft hue had become so normal to me that I'd forgotten how vibrant it'd once been, back before the three miscarriages that triggered her depression.

In some ways, I still blamed myself for not realizing what was happening. Sometimes I worried that my dad blamed me, too, that that's why he didn't care to hear about my aura reading anymore. Because if I had used my gift like I should have, I would have known something was wrong with her. I would have seen the dark haze following her each day. I would have known when she called herself a bad mother that those weren't her words, that there was a darker force feeding off her soul's energy, eating away at it until there was nothing left.

Why hadn't I noticed it with Camden? *Maybe I just didn't want to see it,* I thought to myself. He didn't *seem* depressed. I realized then that should have been my first clue.

The more I thought about it, though, the more the pieces seemed to fall into place. His loss of appetite at lunch, the headaches he said he got... That year of basketball he skipped had to have been because he'd lost interest, not because he wasn't good enough. Then there was that thing he'd said earlier. *Sometimes I wonder if maybe they'd be better off without me around.* I should have known better than to brush that off. I should have known better than to brush *any* of it off. This was all on me, all because I didn't want to see the truth that was staring me in the face. Because if I had admitted what was happening, I'd have to face the memories of my mother's death *again,* and even now, I didn't want to have to do that.

The memory of the day they found her flashed through my mind. I'd come home from school to find police cars and an ambulance in my driveway. Dad held me as I cried into his arms after he told me what happened. I'd seen the dark haze—the demon—emerging from the house. It was obvious at that point because he'd become so strong.

"Katie." Camden's voice pulled me from my thoughts. "What is all this?" He gestured to my spell book and candle on the table.

I didn't answer for several seconds. How did I tell him my mom had taught me how to read auras and cast spells? Instead, I settled for, "It's a way to get rid of it."

He eyed me skeptically. "Look, I'm sorry about what happened to your mom, but I don't believe in this kind of stuff—demons or whatever. You can't help me." The red aura I'd seen earlier had faded to almost nothing.

I glanced toward the dark haze beside him. "That's how it wants you to feel. It wants you to feel worthless, like you can't be saved. It's been, what? A year? Give or take? I *know* about this stuff. Let me help you." The truth was, I didn't know *that* much about it. I'd never cast a protection spell over someone else, and certainly never to protect them from a *demon*. But I had to at least try.

Camden narrowed his eyes skeptically. "How could you know?"

"My mom. She—"

"I mean about me. No one at Aurora High was

supposed to know. This was supposed to be my fresh start."

I shifted on my knees in front of the coffee table. "No one told me, Camden. You think after watching my mom go through the same thing for two years that I wouldn't recognize the signs?"

I instantly felt sick. I hated using that as an explanation because it wasn't true. You never got used to seeing it. At first, you see it everywhere. The depression. The demons. The memories. Then you become so used to seeing it where it's not that you have no choice but to brush it off or rationalize it as something else. Only, I'd done that one too many times.

Camden fidgeted on the couch, and his voice rose slightly like he was scared. "How could you know when I didn't even know for the longest time? I watched my brother go through it, and I couldn't even tell when the same thing was happening to me."

It took me a moment to realize what he was saying. The death in his family that he'd mentioned…it was his older brother.

I dropped my gaze to my hands and spoke quietly. "That's the thing about suicide, Camden. It doesn't end the pain. It just hands it off to someone else."

I surprised even myself with the revelation. Could it

be that the demon attached to him was the same one that'd been attached to his brother? It made sense.

Tears rose to Camden's eyes. "My brother was my best friend. I mean, sure, we fought, but after he punched Jared Novak for making fun of my braces when I was twelve, we really grew together. Brandon had no filter and thought he knew best, but I always thought he was the one constant in my life." He wrung his hands together in his lap.

I suspected he was talking more for his own benefit than for mine, but soon, he went quiet. The urge to fill the silence consumed me. I had to get him to believe me. If he didn't, I may not be able to help him.

"Demons look for weaknesses in your aura, your soul's energy," I explained. "They feed off the weakest of us in their most vulnerable times. I'm guessing for you it was right after your brother died. It saw you as an easy target."

I couldn't tell if Camden was listening to me or lost in his own mind. I wanted to continue, but before I could, the sound of my father's footsteps on the front steps reached my ears.

"Shit," I muttered under my breath as I gathered my book and candle in my hands and shoved them under the couch in record time. I plopped down next to Camden before my dad made it into the living room.

Dad glanced between Camden and me. We both stood.

"Hi, Dad. This is, uh, Camden."

The confusion on his face deepened. No doubt he was wondering why I'd brought the "weird" guy over. And he was probably shocked to see a guy at our house at all. It wasn't exactly a common occurrence, but it's not like he had any rules against it. He never had a reason to.

"Hello, sir," Camden said, stretching out his hand.

Dad shook it and muttered a greeting. Then he turned to me. "Are you going to Briana's today?"

I'd nearly forgotten it was Friday. "Yes," I answered almost too quickly. "I put a roast in the crock pot for you. It should be done soon."

He nodded, but I could see the fatigue in his body after a long week at work. His shoulders fell, and his eyes drooped.

"Okay," Dad said, passing by us and falling to the couch. He crossed his ankles and closed his eyes. "You two have fun."

I bit my lip nervously, glancing at my dad and then to the floor where my spell book lay beneath the couch. I needed it if I was going to help Camden.

"We should maybe get going," Camden suggested.

I glanced at him with a look that told him to give me

a minute. My dad's eyes remained closed so *maybe* there was a chance I could get the book and hurry out the door without him noticing. My heart pounded as I inched closer to the couch. Dad didn't seem to notice. Slowly, I eased my way onto my knees. Before I could reach underneath the couch for the book, his eyes shot open. Thinking fast, I leaned over to give him a hug.

"Bye, Dad. I'll see you later."

He squeezed me back. "Bye."

Before I stood, I caught one more glance at his closed eyes and decided to make my move then. I slid my hand beneath the couch until it fell around the corners of the book, and I snatched it up. I held it tightly to my chest while following behind Camden to his car, grabbing my purse by the door on my way.

As I slid into the passenger seat, my pulse finally returned to normal. I let out a breath of relief. "So, Camden, are you going to let me help you or not?"

CHAPTER NINE

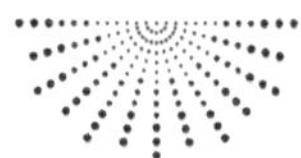

*C*amden started down the street before answering. His words came through clenched teeth. "I told you. You can't help me."

"And I told you, that's what it wants you to think."

Camden shook his head. His frustration was palpable. "This is crazy. I can't have demon attached to me. Demons aren't real."

"Another thing it wants you to think."

Camden's voice rose, surprising me. "Why do you care anyway?" He sucked in a long breath and stared out the window.

It took me a few seconds to answer. When I did, my voice came out small. "Because I don't want one of my friends to get hurt."

Camden looked at me so long that I had the urge to tell him to keep his eyes on the road.

Worry knotted in my chest. What could I possibly say to him? I needed him to go into this willingly or I'd never be able to help him. Could I mention how he was only mad because I'd upset the demon attached to him? Could I tell him how that tension in the air wasn't just between us, that it was his soul energy being sucked away by the dark haze he couldn't see in the back seat? I cursed myself again for not noticing that the darkness I'd seen surrounding him earlier wasn't his aura.

Silence stretched between us. There was no way I could *prove* any of this to him.

"Camden." My voice broke the stillness in the car, sounding strange even to me. "Didn't you say I was the first girl you noticed at Aurora High?"

"Yeah. So?"

"Maybe there's a reason for that. Maybe it's because I can help you."

He sighed but didn't speak.

"Don't you want help?" The words didn't come out accusatory, but I could tell the moment I said them that I'd hit a nerve.

Camden flinched. "You think I want to feel like this? I moved here to get a fresh start. I made an effort. I tried making friends and having fun, and—" He choked up before he could finish, but I could still sense the meaning behind his words. *And it didn't help.*

My heart dropped. He'd tried so hard to push the pain away and hide it from the rest of us. It was one of the reasons I hadn't noticed. Even now that I knew he was struggling, I couldn't understand the extent of what he'd been through.

"If there was a chance that someone could help you, wouldn't you want to take that chance?" I stared at him, willing him to accept my help. When he didn't speak, I had no choice but to try harder. "Look, you may not believe me, but if I'm wrong, I'll do whatever I can to find a solution that *will* help you. So please, just let me try this. What could it hurt?"

Camden's expression softened. He glanced at me, and I knew he couldn't miss the desperation and urgency written all over my face. I couldn't lose another person I had a chance to help. I just couldn't.

He let out a wavering breath but nodded. Without saying anything, he flipped on his blinker and turned down the next street. I didn't bother asking why we were no longer headed to Briana's. I didn't want him to change his mind.

A few minutes later, we pulled up to his house. The small one-story white building was familiar since I'd visited Austin's next door several times throughout the years, but it was strange walking through the lawn for the first time. Instead of leading me to the front door, however, Camden rounded the side of the house. I held my spell book close to my chest as I followed behind him.

"Are your grandparents home?" I asked, feeling strangely like I was intruding.

"No. They keep busy. Will this work?" Camden stopped at the base of a tree and pointed to the treehouse just feet above our heads.

I nodded. It was small and private. "It's perfect."

I climbed into the treehouse and crossed my legs on the aged wooden floor. Aside from a broken stool in the corner and the occasional leaf, the place was empty. Camden sat across from me, our knees nearly touching in the small space.

"So, uh," he spoke slowly. "How is this going to work?"

I opened the book and flipped to the page I needed. I scanned the top of the page. First, we were supposed to cleanse the space. I didn't have any herbs with me, so I hoped we could skip that step and it would still work. The thing was, I didn't want to stop now and gather the supplies. I worried Camden wouldn't be up for it the longer he had to consider my offer. Since he brought me to the treehouse, I imagined it was already a fairly cleansed space, somewhere he felt safe and happy. If this place was filled with happy memories, and I suspected it was, this may just work.

"This is more about you than me," I admitted. "It starts by cleansing your aura, and that works by focusing on happy thoughts and memories. I know it's hard, but you have to be willing to let go of your anger and frustration."

Camden let out a breath of disbelief. He hardly seemed like the confident guy I'd thought he was. I realized now that had been an act. He'd been trying to be the person he *wanted* to be, and unless we could cleanse him of this demon, he'd never become that person. Camden didn't mention again how strange and silly this all seemed to him, but I could tell by the look on his face he still wasn't buying it.

I closed the book, marking the spot with my pointer finger. "Let's try something else. Forget about the book. Forget about everything I told you. Tell me about this treehouse."

"What?" Camden asked with a forced laugh.

"Why'd you bring me here?" I attempted a friendly tone.

He shrugged.

"You like this place, don't you?"

He shrugged again. "I guess."

"What do you like about it?"

Camden's shoulders relaxed. "Nostalgia."

"What's one of your favorite memories here?" I gestured around me.

Getting off the topic of demons and depression seemed to help Camden relax. He now spoke as he had earlier when we'd been getting to know each other. It was like we were actually friends now.

"I remember building it with my grandpa and my brother," he said, a smile creeping onto his face. "I was seven, and Brandon was nine. We spent two weeks here over the summer. It was one of the best summers of my life."

I smiled back at him. "That's cool. What'd you use the treehouse for?"

As Camden recounted stories from his childhood, I pulled in deep, long breaths and let the tension in my shoulders release with every exhale. The more I did it, the more relaxed I noticed he became. He mimicked my deep breathing without noticing. It was a trick I'd learned from my mom. She'd do the same thing to me when I was angry or upset. I never noticed until my dad pointed it out.

"I'm going to read from my book now," I told Camden once he seemed relaxed enough. "But don't stop telling me stories, okay? I'm still listening."

Camden shot me a questioning look, but he didn't say anything. Instead, he continued his story about the summer he'd gone to the county fair with his grandpa and brother. The more he talked about them, the more I realized how much they both meant to him. It made his loss only that much more difficult to swallow.

I opened the book to the page I'd marked with my finger and began chanting the incantation under my breath. A chill breeze passed through the treehouse when I read the second line, rustling the pages of my spell book.

Camden's voice ceased mid-sentence, and his eyes grew wide.

"It's okay," I told him, but the breeze freaked even me out. I eyed the dark haze beside him. It was so close to him now, and I knew it had to be influencing him in ways I couldn't sense, placing doubt and fear in his mind. "So, what happened after you got cotton candy?"

Camden relaxed once again and continued his story.

I restarted the incantation, glancing up every now and then to monitor the haze beside him. The further into the spell I got, the darker, more prominent the demon's aura became. I had pissed it off big time. There was no turning back now.

By the time I reached the end of the incantation, nothing had happened. It didn't surprise me that it would take a few tries as I'd never performed this spell before. Plus, I wasn't entirely sure Camden was at a point himself to help in warding off the demon. I returned my eyes to the top of the page and restarted. Camden didn't seem to notice.

By the third time through the incantation, I glanced up and noticed a barely visible blue hue around Camden. Excitement sizzled through me. Camden's stories were helping strengthen his aura while my incantation was weakening the demon's bond on him. The brighter his aura grew, the dimmer the haze beside him became.

I couldn't help it when my voice rose during the fifth time through the incantation. Confidence flowed through me as I reached the last few lines. The haze shrank into a small ball. *This is it,* I thought.

But just as I reached the last line, Camden paused. His blue aura dimmed slightly as the dark one beside him began to expand again.

"Tell me more," I insisted. "What's your happiest memory? Tell me about your first kiss." I returned the incantation, repeating it for the sixth time as Camden spoke.

He gazed down at his hands. I continued to watch the dark haze, but I didn't miss the blush that rose to his cheeks.

"Well, it wasn't my first one, but it was the best."

I nodded, encouraging him to continue all without stopping or taking my eyes off the haze.

"I'd just met this incredible girl. Dark hair, pretty eyes. There was just something about her. I wanted to get to know her. So I took her on a hike, and when we got back to the car, she let me kiss her. Something about the kiss...it just...made me feel something real for the first time in forever. I—I want to feel that again."

It was only a split second after finishing the last word in the incantation that I realized what he was saying. He was talking about *our* kiss. I didn't get a chance to pull in another breath before he swiftly closed the distance between us, completely taking me off guard.

Camden's lips locked on mine. One arm came around to rest on my hip and the other on the back of my neck. In that moment, the kiss was all that seemed to matter. I forgot about the spell book. I forgot about the demon. That kiss was all there was.

Eventually, the rational part of my mind took hold again. I drew away from his chest and attempted to catch my breath. This wasn't the answer. This feeling, this passion, it was only temporary. Before I could find the words to tell him so, he pulled me back into him. Camden rose to his knees, pulling me up with him until our bodies collided. Warmth flowed through me like an electric current. I closed my eyes, melting into his embrace, and my heart hammered against my chest so hard I was sure he could feel it.

The spell book fell from my lap onto the floor beside me with a thud, snapping me back to reality. Camden's lips remained on mine, but my eyes shot open to fall on the dark haze beside him. The outline of the demon's aura seemed to grow more defined and dense. I hugged Camden tighter.

He's mine, I shouted in my mind.

The demon's aura seemed to shrink into a small black ball until it appeared as if I could reach out and touch it. It was like it wasn't just a ball of energy anymore but was a physical object.

You can't have him. Not this time.

My lips pressed more forcefully against Camden's. A split second later, the ball of energy exploded, sending a strong gust of wind throughout the treehouse. My hair flew out of my face, and I had to close my eyes to keep dust particles from landing in them.

I jumped away from Camden in surprise. My pulse raced, but it quickly slowed. Camden didn't seem to notice the gust of wind wasn't an ordinary breeze. I relaxed back into his embrace. I kept my eyes locked on where the dark haze had just vanished from, but it was finally gone.

Camden had been right about our kiss making him feel something. That calm, blue aura I'd seen before had been replaced by a bright, vibrant red. The newfound strength in his aura coupled with my incantation had worked. I beamed. Maybe intimacy wasn't the answer, but I knew it had been more than that. I'd showed him I was willing to help him, and maybe it shifted his perspective just enough to give him a sliver of hope.

"What?" he asked softly.

I stared into his icy blue eyes. The words eluded me as I once again brought my lips to meet his.

EPILOGUE

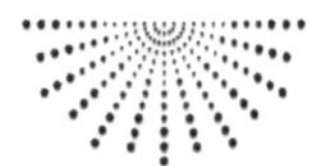

Camden still didn't believe my spell book had saved him, even weeks later. He didn't notice the change right away, but I could see his aura growing brighter and brighter by the day. He claimed it was our friendship that brought about the change, but I knew better. Camden still had a lot of emotional baggage to work through, but he was slowly making progress. The first step had been getting rid of the demon feeding off his energy. The next step was facing his past.

Camden and I stepped out of the car. Small snowflakes fluttered through the air. It felt great to stretch my legs after the long car ride. I had the urge to wrap my arms around myself tighter for warmth in the chilly breeze, but I much preferred to hold onto Camden's hand. He transferred the bouquet of flowers to his left hand and squeezed mine with his right. The more grave markers we passed, the tighter his hold became.

"Hey," I said softly, stopping him. I could already see the tears rising to his eyes. "I'm here for you."

Camden nodded. "I know."

"Take as much time as you need."

He cracked a shy smile. "Thanks, but I'm okay. Let me go introduce you to my brother."

Camden led me down the next row of grave stones. He stopped in front of a granite one etched with Brandon Cooper's name on it.

"Hey, Brandon." Camden's words caught in his throat.

He released my hand and instead wrapped his arm around me, pulling me close. Together, we knelt, and he placed his flowers on the headstone. After a few moments, Camden choked out another word I couldn't quite make out then pressed his free hand to his eyes.

"I miss you so much." His voice cracked.

I couldn't do anything but draw even closer to him to let him know I was there. He wasn't alone in this.

Camden swallowed deeply. "There's not a day I don't think about you, Brandon. You were my best friend. Nothing will ever be the same without you."

I entwined my fingers in his and squeezed tight.

"This is Katie, by the way," Camden told his brother. "She, um, she's helping me… She's helping me see the good about your life instead of the bad about your death. And I'm doing better. I hope you are, too. Because one day we're going to meet again, and I want to see that smile on your face when we do."

I pulled away from Camden to shoot him a smile of encouragement. I noticed that his aura had grown brighter than when we'd stepped out of the car, as if he finally felt at peace. Relaxing back into his embrace, I glanced around the cemetery. I wondered if maybe since I'd seen the demon's aura if I had the power to see his brother's too. I didn't, but there was no doubt in my mind that Brandon heard every word Camden said to him.

On the drive home, Camden recounted stories about him and Brandon. Some of them I'd heard before, but I sat patiently and listened to them again. I didn't know if it happened at the cemetery or somewhere along the car ride home, but when Camden dropped me off at home that night, I had this strange feeling that his pain had finally melted away.

ABOUT THE AUTHOR

Alicia Rades is a USA Today bestselling author of young adult and new adult paranormal fiction. When she's not dreaming up magical stories, she's either binge-watching paranormal TV shows, meditating, or spending time with her family. She has an unhealthy obsession with psychic characters and writes with a deck of tarot cards next to her computer.